Shout!

Little Poems that Roar

by
**Brod
Bagert**

illustrated by
**Sachiko
Yoshikawa**

Dial Books for Young Readers

SHOUT

Shout it! Shout it! **POETRY!**
Fun for you and fun for me.

Clap your hands! Stomp your feet!
Feel the rhythm! Feel the beat!

Chunky words all chopped in chips!
Silky sounds upon your lips.

Tell a story—happy, sad;
Silly, sorry; good or bad.

Leap a leap, hop a hop,
See the ocean in one drop.

Shout it! Shout it! **POETRY!**
Fun for you and fun for me.

KIDS RULE!

Write your letters—
So much fun!
Off to gym class—
RUN! RUN! RUN!

Time for numbers—
One and two!
Now it's lunchtime—
CHEW! CHEW! CHEW!

Out for recess—
Kid stampede!
In for stories—
READ! READ! READ!

Work and play all day at SCHOOL—
KIDS LEARN!
KIDS RULE!

THE LIBRARY CHEER

Books are good!
Books are great!
I want books!
I **WILL NOT WAIT!**
  Bird books,
  Bug books,
  Bear books too,
  Words and pictures
  Through and through.

Books are good!
Books are great!
I want books!
I **WILL NOT WAIT!**
  Books in color,
  Black and white,
  Skinny books,
  Fat books,
  Day and night.

Books are good!
Books are great!
I want books!
I **WILL NOT WAIT!**
  Sad books,
  Glad books,
  Funny books too,
  Books for me
  And books for you.

Books are good!
Books are great!
I want books!
I **WILL NOT WAIT!**

THE LEARNER

Two plus two is twenty-three.
It's not, you say? Oh no, poor me.

Two plus two is . . . seventy-eight?
I'll get it right if you'll just wait.

Two plus two is . . . forty-one?
Wrong again? This is no fun.

Two plus two . . . is . . . thirty-two?
Adding seems so hard to do.

Two plus two . . . I think . . . is . . . four?
That's right? Hurraaaaaay!
Let's add some more.

OUR CLASSROOM ZOO

Kitty whiskers, kitty feet,
Kitty sounds are soft and sweet.
Meow.

Moo-cows standing all around,
Listen to the moo-cow sound.
Moooo . . . Moooo . . .
Meow.

Puppies pouncing playfully,
Why do puppies bark at me?
RUFF! RUFF! RUFF!
Moooo . . . Moooo . . .
Meow.

Every day the rooster crows,
This is how the rooster goes—
COCK-A-DOODLE-DOO!
RUFF! RUFF! RUFF!
Moooo . . . Moooo . . .
Meow.

Monkey tail, monkey hair,
Monkeys climbing everywhere.
SCREECH! SCREECH!
COCK-A-DOODLE-DOO!
RUFF! RUFF! RUFF!
Moooo . . . Moooo . . .
Meow.

Our classroom sounds
just like a zoo.
WATCH OUT FOR THAT KANGAROO!

Boing!

SNACK TIME

Cake and cookies,
Cookies and cake,
Now it's time
To take a break.
  Cake in my hand,
  Cake in my tummy.
  Snack time is so
  YUMMY, **YUMMY!**

Chips and pretzels,
Pretzels and chips,
Feels so salty
On my lips.
  Chips in my hand,
  Chips in my tummy.
  Snack time is so
  YUMMY, **YUMMY!**

Cheese and crackers,
Crackers and cheese,
You can have some
If you please.
  Cheese in my hand,
  Cheese in my tummy.
  Snack time is so
  YUMMY, **YUMMY!**

Such a mess!
Filthy room!
Get a dustpan,
Get a broom.
  Wipe the table,
  Sweep the floor,
  GET SOME SNACKS AND EAT SOME MORE!

QUACK

Quack.

Quack, quack.

Quack-quack-quack.

Quack-quack,
Quack-quack-quack,
Quack-quack-quack-quack,
Quack-quack!

"Stop . . . that . . . QUACKING!"

(Quack.)

BIG FAT HEN

I can count from one to ten.
Big fat hen!
Big fat hen!

I can do it with a friend.
Big fat hen!
Big fat hen!

Here we go, let's count again.
Big fat hen!
Big fat hen!

1 . . . 2 . . . 3 . . .
BIG!
4 . . . 5 . . . 6 . . . 9 . . .
FAT! 7 . . . 8 . . . 9
HEN!
10!
Big fat hen.

TAKING TURNS

Summer sunshine, summer heat,
Summer sandals on my feet.
Lots of time for me to play,
Summer, please don't go away.

Autumn, autumn—turning cool.
Time for me to go to school.
Something tingles in the air . . .
I see pumpkins everywhere!

Winter, winter—ice and snow,
Bundle up from head to toe.
Snow at sunset, snow at dawn,
Soon the snow will all be gone.

Springtime! Springtime! Spring is here!
Springtime flowers make me cheer!
Springtime showers, warm and clean,
Everything I see is green!

Every year, it's only fair,
All the seasons have to share,
All the seasons have to learn
That every season takes a turn.

MY SHADOW

The coolest thing you'll ever see
Is how my shadow follows me.
Front or back, left or right,
My shadow is a friendly sight.
Sometimes big, sometimes small,
My shadow loves me most of all.

Every single sunny day,
The two of us go out to play.
Front or back, left or right,
My shadow is a friendly sight.
Sometimes big, sometimes small,
My shadow loves me most of all.

The only time it's out of sight
Is in a room without a light.
Front or back, left or right,
My shadow is a friendly sight.
Sometimes big, sometimes small,
My shadow loves me most of all.

I have a shadow of my own
And so I never feel alone.
Front or back, left or right,
My shadow is my heart's delight.
Sometimes big, sometimes small,
My shadow loves me most of all.

SCARECROW EYES

I shut my eyes, I shut them tight,
That scarecrow was a scary sight—
Scary body! Scary face!
My classroom was a scary place.

But then I looked and soon I saw,
That scarecrow was all stuffed with straw!
Straw-stuffed body . . . Straw-stuffed face . . .
My classroom was a happy place.

Giggle, giggle with delight,
A scarecrow is a scary sight,
But if you look and do not run
You'll see that scarecrows can be **fun.**

PLAY TIME

We play with books, we play with clay,
We play with colors, red and gray.
We run to school, we don't delay,
Because at school we get to play.
    PLAY! PLAY! PLAY! PLAY!
    HOW WE CHILDREN LOVE TO PLAY!

We children really need to play,
We cannot live the grown-up way.
Someday we'll have to work all day,
But now it's time for us to play.
    PLAY! PLAY! PLAY! PLAY!
    HOW WE CHILDREN LOVE TO PLAY!

We play with colors, red and gray,
We play with books, we play with clay.
Our favorite part of every day,
Is when we go outside to play.
    PLAY! PLAY! PLAY! PLAY!

    PLAY! PLAY! PLAY! PLAY!

    PLAY! PLAY! PLAY! PLAY!

    HOW WE CHILDREN LOVE TO PLAY!
Yeah . . .

FINGER PAINTS

Finger paint, finger paint,
Everyplace.
Start with paper,
Paint a face.
Paint some ears,
Paint some hair,
Finger paint, finger paint,
Everywhere!

Finger paint, finger paint,
Paint a door,
Paint a ceiling,
Paint a floor.
Paint a window,
Wide and high,
Look right through
And paint a sky.

Finger paint, finger paint,
Paint a sun,
Paint some clouds,
So much fun!
Sun comes up,
Sun goes down.
Finger paint, finger paint,
All around!

Hang your paintings,
From a hook.
Everyone
Will take a look.
All the earth
In green and blue,
All the world
Right out of you.

THE SPICE OF LIFE

Ketchup, ketchup on my fries,
Oh so pretty to my eyes,
On my fingers, on my face,
I like ketchup everyplace.
    Ketchup chips, ketchup cheese,
    Ketchup soup, ketchup peas,
    Ketchup dogs with ketchup fleas,
    Give me ketchup if you please.

Listen now to what I say,
This could be a perfect day,
Oh, the strength! Oh, the power!
Let me take a ketchup shower.
    Ketchup cheese, ketchup chips,
    Ketchup lipstick on my lips,
    Ketchup peas, ketchup soup,
    Gooey, gooey, ketchup goop!

I like ketchup, thick and nice,
Ketchup is a perfect spice.
KETCHUP!

KETCHUP!

KETCHUP!

WIND, RAIN, AND SUNSHINE

Sandbox, sandbox, windy place,
Sand on my shoulders, sand on my face.
Sand in my ears, sand in my hair,
Sand is blowing everywhere!

Sandbox, sandbox, rainy day,
Raindrops wash the sand away.
Castle walls . . . looking bad . . .
Raindrops make the sandbox sad.

Sandbox drying in the sun,
Sunshine makes the sandbox fun.
Sand in a bucket, sand in a cup,
Sand in my shoes when I get up.

NO FEAR

T. rex, T. rex, big and tall.
Meanest monster of them all.

Pterodactyl in the sky.
Holy mackerel! It can fly!

Stegosaurus, what a shock,
Armor plate as hard as rock!

DINOSAUR PARK

Brontosaurus, fancy-free.
Holy smoke! It ate a tree!

Megaraptor! Giant jaws!
Giant teeth! Giant claws!

Dinosaurs I do not fear
Because they are no longer here.

May is here!
Almost June!
Summer! Summer!
Coming soon!
    Four-leaf clover,
    Make a wish!
    Bounce a beach ball,
    Catch a fish.

I CAN'T WAIT

May is here!
Almost June!
Summer! Summer!
Coming soon!
    Ride a skateboard,
    Ride a bike,
    Throw that baseball,
    It's a strike!

May is here!
Almost June!
Summer! Summer!
Coming soon!
    How much longer?
    What's the date?
    Summer! Summer!
I CAN'T WAIT!

ALPHABET BOOGIE

I can **do it**,

Yes-sir-ee,
I'm as smart
As I can be.

A . . . Yes.
B . . . Yes.
C . . . **Yes.**
Deeeeeeeeeee!
I can do it!
Yes-sir-ee!

E-F-G!
H-I-J!
Wait, there's more,
Don't run away.

Here's a K
With an
L-M-N-O-P!
Q-R-S
And a T-U-V!

Next comes W,
X-Y-Z.
I'm as smart
As I can be!

Put that pencil
In my hand.
I can do it,

YES I CAN!

SENSE ALIVE

Senses, senses, I have five,
Senses make me feel alive.
　Everybody look at me,
　I have eyes that let me see.

Senses, senses, I have five,
Senses make me feel alive.
　Listen, listen, I can hear
　Giggle noises in my ear.

Senses, senses, I have five,
Senses make me feel alive.
　I can touch, I can feel,
　Everything I touch is real.

Senses, senses, I have five,
Senses make me feel alive.
　I want candy, I can't wait,
　Chocolate candy tastes so great.

Senses, senses, I have five,
Senses make me feel alive.
　In the bathroom Daddy goes . . .
　WISH I DIDN'T HAVE A NOSE!

Senses, senses, I have five,
Senses make me feel **ALIVE!**

TEDDY BEAR

In bed he doesn't have a care
Because he has his teddy bear.

He whispers oh so soft and low,
"Teddy Bear, I love you so."

He knows it's just a little strange
But I don't think he'll ever change.

I have just one more thing to add,
I wrote this poem about my dad.

LITTLE DIPPER

Little Dipper in the sky,
Little Dipper, please don't cry.
Not as bright as all the rest?
Brightness doesn't make them best.

All the others move around,
Always on the roam.
You stay right there in the north
And point the way back home.

Little Dipper in the sky,
Little Dipper, please don't cry.
Small you are . . . yet still you stay,
And that is how I find my way.